HERE'S WHAT KIDS SAY ABOUT BOOKS IN THE
EARTH INSPECTORS™ SERIES!

"I felt like I was right there."   —Derek Smith

"Very futuristic, exciting and even funny."
—Elizabeth Minet

"So good I didn't want to put it down."
—Amy Greene

"While you're having fun...you're learning also."
—Danielle Becker

"Exciting...full of surprises."   —Tim Ferris

"I give it an A + ."   —Simon Smith

Books in the EARTH INSPECTORS ™ Series

EARTH INSPECTORS™

9

EUROPE

Why was a city built to capture a castle?

by Sara Compton

Illustrations by Barbara Carter

McGRAW-HILL PUBLISHING COMPANY

New York   St. Louis   San Francisco   Auckland   Bogotá   Hamburg
London   Madrid   Mexico   Milan   Montreal   New Delhi
Paris   São Paulo   Singapore   Sydney   Tokyo   Toronto

1 2 3 4 5 6 7 8 9   SEM   SEM   9 5 4 3 2 1 0

ISBN 0-07-048003-6

LIBRARY OF CONGRESS CATALOGING-IN-PUBLICATION DATA

Compton, Sara
   Europe: Why was a city built to capture a castle? / by Sara Compton
      p. cm.
—(Earth inspectors; 9)   Summary: As an Earth Inspector, the reader
makes an exciting journey through medieval European castles among
knights, serfs, dukes, and the future Queen of France.
   ISBN 0-07-048003-6
   1. Plot-your-own stories.   [1. Middle Ages—Fiction.
2. Time travel—Fiction.   3. Plot-your-own stories]   I. Title.   II. Series
PZ7.C7365Eu   1989   [Fic]   89-12729
[Fic]—dc19   CIP
                                                                AC

Dear Reader,

Are there really aliens in outer space? Most scientists think it likely. And many people have tried to guess what they would be like.

If they were very intelligent and had invented spaceships, they might want to see what's happening here. After all, Earth is a very interesting planet.

Imagine how an alien would feel, after traveling trillions of miles in a spacecraft, to see a beautiful blue-white sphere growing larger and larger in the star-studded black sky.

Imagine *you* are that alien—one living on Turoc, a planet far more advanced than ours—that you are an Earth Inspector!

Edward Packard

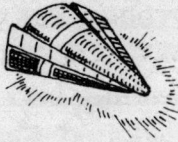

It's a calm day on the Sea of Turoc. The waves gently rolling toward the pink sand are only about thirty feet tall. Perfect conditions for skyboarding, you think, as you lounge on the smooth surface of your board, waiting to catch the next wave.

"Heads up!" The voice comes from Zy, a fellow Earth Inspector.

"Uh-oh!" Another Earth Inspector, Shala, is close enough so you can see her enormous eyes shining with excitement.

The three of you ready your skyboards for the biggest wave of the day. It must be forty feet tall! The glassy green wall looms behind you. Lying on your stomach, you paddle furiously, then you scramble to your feet as you feel your skyboard pick up speed. You shoot along the glassy water inside the curl of the wave, expertly balancing on your board.

Just before the mighty wave crashes onto the shore, you kick out. Here comes the most exciting part of the ride, as you're launched into the air for another fifty feet of flight before you land in the surf.

"What a ride!" you yell as you spot Shala and Zy nearby.

Zy is already heading back out into the deep water, but you've spotted a mass of dark clouds overhead. "There's a squall coming," you yell.

You watch your friend paddle back to shore. You smile to yourself. What would Zy do without someone like you around to keep him from losing his neck? You remember the time you had to go all the way to the Earth city of Venice to rescue him.

The three of you shake the water off your fur and put your skyboards in the back of Shala's beat-up jet rover. She slides behind the control panel, and you and Zy hop in beside her and fasten your restraints. You feel the jet engines ignite, and soon you're cruising along about a hundred feet above the water, heading for your second home—the Earth Inspector base.

You look down longingly at the big waves.

"They don't have anything like that where you're going," says Shala.

"I saw some waves that big when I was on a mission to Earth," you say. "In Hawaii. They even have a sport something like skyboarding. They call it surfboarding."

"Ever try it?" asks Zy.

"Sure. It feels a lot like skyboarding so long as you're inside the curl of the wave, but there's no sky glide at the end."

"I wouldn't think so," says Shala. "Earth has four times the gravity of our planet. And human Earthlings are four times as heavy!"

Just then a green light fills the cabin of the jet rover, signaling Shala that she has permission to land. You hadn't realized you'd reached your destination, and your thoughts turn to your next mission to Earth. It's an exciting planet, and you wonder what adventures await you as you feel the jet rover glide to a halt.

Go on to the next page.

Ten minutes later you say good-bye to Zy and Shala and enter the Chamber of Wisdom. Simbar, Surveyor of the Spheres, looks very grave as he rises to greet you. Beside him stands a shiny metal suit known to Earthlings as armor. The sight of it sends a shudder down your spine.

"You recognize this?" he asks gently.

"I do," you answer quietly. "It is the suit of armor that Teega was wearing when she returned from her mission to Earth."

Simbar nods and sighs. "As you know, Teega was so badly wounded she could barely talk when she returned to Turoc. By the next day, she was dead." Simbar wipes away a tear. "The only Earth Inspector we've ever lost!"

You put a hand on his shoulder. "You did everything you could to save her."

You can see that Simbar is still trying to recover from the shock of Teega's death—a death that had affected you deeply as well. Teega had been one of the youngest Earth Inspectors. Like most brilliant and talented rookies, she had a reckless streak. But hers was a mile wide.

You had supervised her first mission—to the United States of America. She had been on her first solo assignment when she died.

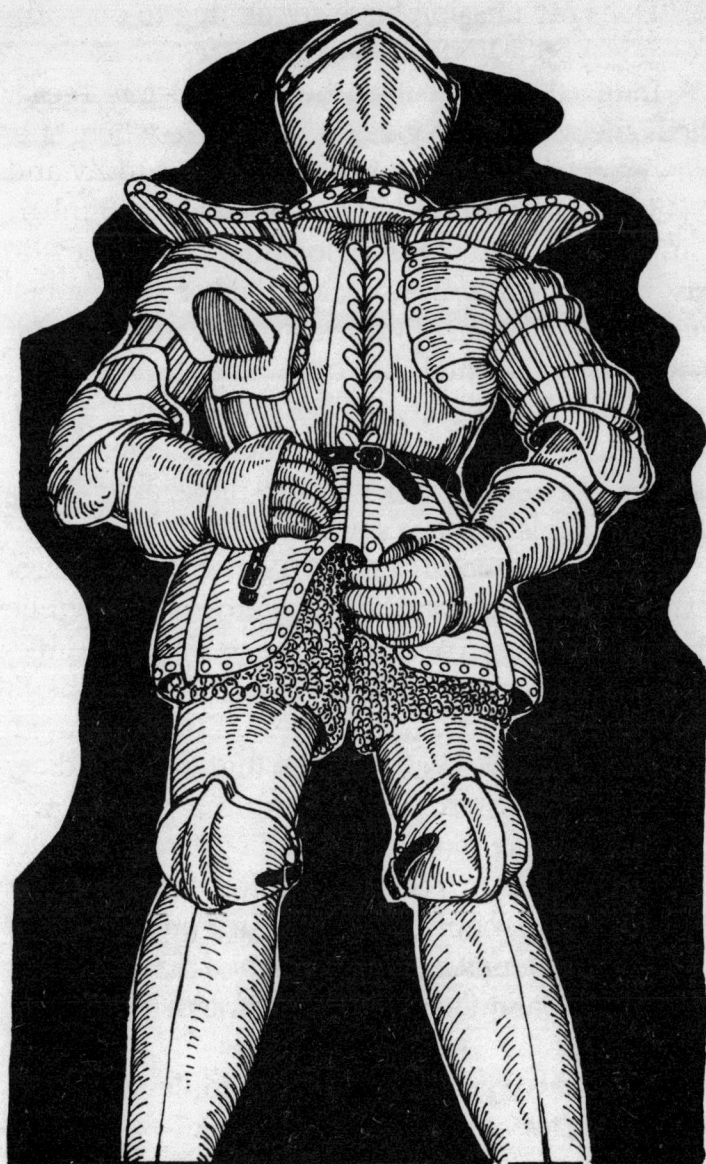

"Does my mission have something to do with Teega?" you ask after a long silence.

"Indirectly, yes," comes the reply. "Before Teega died, she was able to give us a clue as to where she was when she received her fatal wounds."

"It was in Europe, wasn't it?" you say.

"Yes—she had made an awesome discovery—a city built to capture a castle." Simbar shakes his head sadly. "She tried desperately to tell us about it when she returned. But she was so fever-crazed we couldn't make out whether she was in the city or the castle when she received her fatal wounds." Simbar sighs, then looks you in the eye. "I want you to complete Teega's mission."

Simbar pulls down a map. It shows the western part of the Earth continent of Europe. You study the map, trying to remember the name of the little country surrounded by France, Italy, and Germany. You recognize the countries west of them, located on a squarish peninsula—Spain and Portugal.

"Is this the only map of Western Europe we have?" you ask.

"I'm afraid so," is Simbar's reply. "This map was made in 1991—hundreds of years after Teega's mission." He runs a pointer over the map. "A lot of these cities, and even these countries, didn't exist back then."

"We're talking about the Middle Ages of Earth's history, aren't we?" you ask.

N

NORTH SEA

NORWAY

ATLANTIC OCEAN

SCOTLAND

Edinburgh

IRELAND

Dublin

ENGLAND

London

DENMARK

Hamburg

Elbe River

Bremen

NETHERLANDS

Amsterdam

Brussels

BELGIUM

Cologne

Bonn

Paris

Seine River

WEST GERMANY

Rhine

Loire River

Tours

FRANCE

AQUITAINE

Bordeaux

Garonne River

Zurich

SWITZERLAND

AUSTRIA

Lyons

ALPS

ITALY

PYRENEES MTNS.

Rhône R.

Ebro River

Marseille

Corsica

PORTUGAL

Lisbon

Tajo River

Madrid

SPAIN

Barcelona

Sardinia

Rome

Granada

Santa Fe

MEDITERRANEAN SEA

Sicily

MOROCCO

ALGERIA

TUNISIA

0   100   200   300   400   500

MILES

Simbar nods. "Earthlings didn't have strong governments way back then. So to protect themselves, kings and queens and knights lived in enormous castles. Some of them had walls twenty feet thick! It was a time of ferocious combat. Weapons that worked like huge slingshots would fire cannonballs over the castle walls. Sometimes they'd just dig a trench under the wall and hope it would collapse!"

You lift the leg of the suit of armor, testing its weight. "This must weigh sixty pounds! It's hard to see how anyone could walk in something this heavy, let alone wage war," you say.

"The knights who wore this armor rode on strong animals called horses," Simbar tells you. "The animals wore armor, too. During combat, knights would gallop toward each other and try to knock each other off the horses with long sharp weapons—lances."

"That could have been what Teega was doing when she was wounded!"

Simbar sighs. "I've thought of that. I blame myself for Teega's death. I didn't even see to it that she knew how to ride a horse!"

"But you couldn't have," you say. "We don't have anything *like* a horse on Turoc."

"We do now," says Simbar. "You'll meet it tomorrow, when you report for training."

You're dying to ask how Simbar brought a horse all the way from Earth! But he's already turned back to the map. "There were thousands of these huge castles scattered over many parts of the Earth—but a great number of them were in Western Europe." Simbar sighs. "It was a dangerous time for Earthlings. They had to build bigger and bigger castles to protect themselves."

Simbar's eyes seem to glow from within. "Teega was so fascinated with this city. I want you to find out where it is and why it was built."

An exciting thought enters your mind. "If I find this place, I might find Teega! I might even be able to save her from dying."

Simbar shakes his furry head. "We don't even know where this place is, let alone *when* Teega was there!" He puts a hand on your shoulder. "You're one of our most resourceful Earth Inspectors. You just might track her down. But if you find Teega alive, you must promise me one thing, and I warn you it won't be easy."

"What's that?" you ask.

"You know the code. You must not do anything to change the course of history on planet Earth. I cannot say it strongly enough."

"You have my promise," you say.

"Even if it means..." Simbar lets the rest of the sentence hang in the air.

"...choosing to let Teega die," you say, finishing his thought.

Go on to the next page.

The next day you report to Simbar. He's already warned you to expect a grueling two-week training course—and he's advised you to report in the human Earthling form you'll be using as a disguise while you're on your mission.

You stagger a little as you enter the Earth simulator. The artificial gravity is just the same as the gravity on Earth—four times as heavy as what you're used to here on Turoc. You're also struggling to get used to your long Earthling legs. But Simbar is all business as he leads the way to a massive four-legged robot.

"You'll need some unusual physical skills for this mission," he tells you. "As I told you, you'll be visiting Earth during a period when Earthlings got around on horses." He proudly puts a hand on the robot's metal neck. "I've had this robot horse built so you can learn to ride. The Earth Techs who put it together gave it a name—Whirlaway."

Simbar shows you how to put your left foot in a holder called a stirrup, give a little push with the other leg, and swing your body up

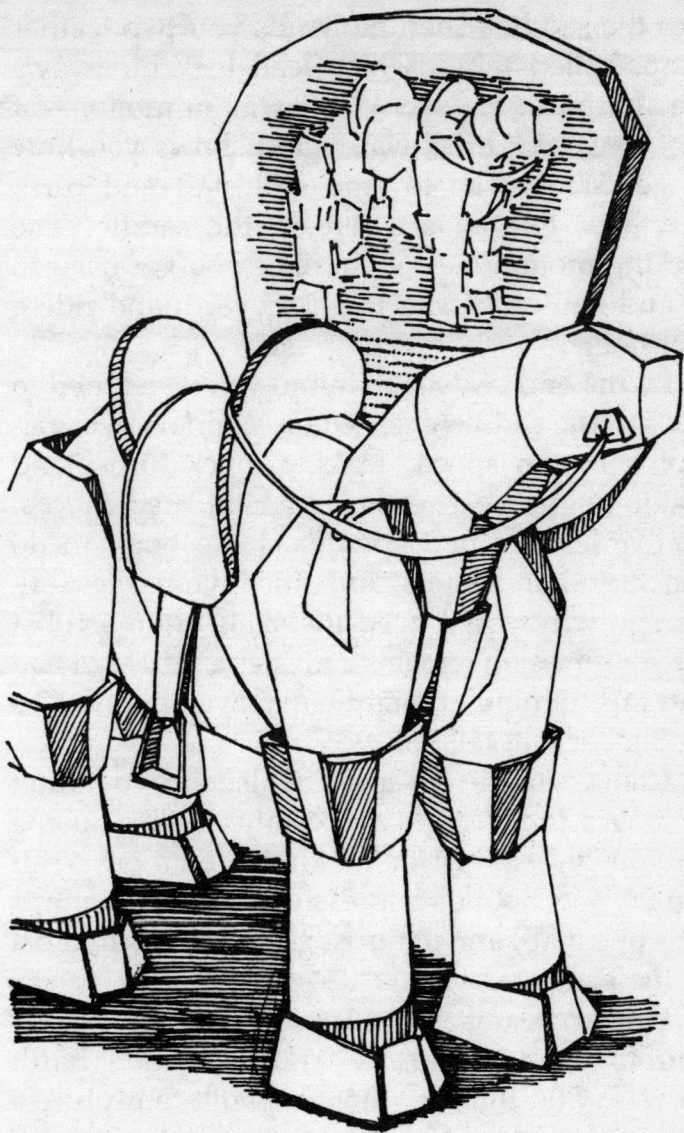

into the saddle. Then he hands you two leather straps called reins, which lead to Whirlaway's metal mouth. He sets Whirlaway in motion—at first, only at a brisk walk—and shows you how to get Whirlaway to stop and start and turn, and how to stay securely in the saddle. The rocking motion feels great once you get used to it, and you can't wait to get to Earth and ride a real horse.

By the end of your training, you've learned to stick to the saddle even when Whirlaway is galloping at top speed, making quick turns, and making simulated leaps over simulated fences. You've also trained your Earthling body to do backflips, handstands, and other gymnastics—although why you'll need the skills of an acrobat for your mission remains a mystery. "If Teega had had this training, it might have saved her life," is all Simbar will tell you.

Chin Chin, the advanced intelligence computer on board the *Voyager* spacecraft you'll be using on your mission is fed all known data on Western Europe. Sounds impressive, but all it amounts to is one map, and a tourist guidebook with most of the pages missing.

Simbar beams with approval as he escorts you to the launchpad. "You've trained hard. Now go find that city that was built to capture a castle!"

You bid farewell, climb into the cockpit of your spacecraft, activate Chin Chin, and issue the command: *"Transit."* Then you give yourself over to the purest joy of all—the thrill of feeling the powerful *Voyager* engines lift you into space and hurl you into the stratosphere.

As soon as you're free of Turoc's gravitational pull, you enter the space–time continuum. "Chin Chin," you say, "set your course for Earth year 1136."

"Brilliant choice of year!" says Chin Chin. "Western Europe, where we're heading, had thousands of working castles back then."

"I want to start my mission by studying one of them up close," you say. "Once I know what goes on inside, I'll have a better chance of figuring out why a city was built to capture a castle, and where I might find it."

Just then you feel a slight jolt as the *Voyager* enters Earth's atmosphere. Outside your cockpit window, you see the Iberian peninsula, the westernmost part of Europe where Spain and Portugal are located. The *Voyager* levels off and streaks across the peninsula, then over France and Germany, ending its flyover in a graceful arc that takes you over Switzerland and Italy. It's a breathtaking ride, as castle after castle comes into view. Many of them are built on the tops of hills, or on the banks of rivers. Some

have little villages grouped around the castle walls.

"Take your pick," says Chin Chin.

He swoops over a good-sized city. You can make out several grand castles.

"That's Paris, home of Louis VI, king of France," he informs you. "They call him Louis the Fat. He loves to eat. In fact, he's gotten so fat he can't even get on a horse!"

You shake your head. You never know what odd fact Chin Chin will come up with.

"Do you have any *hard* data on King Louis?" you ask.

Chin Chin makes the metallic whispery sounds that mean he's searching through his memory. "Here's something," he says after a few seconds. "Louis is more like a major overlord than a king. You don't have to go far from Paris to find powerful dukes and counts ruling their own territory. They're loyal to the king up to a point, but they make their own decisions."

"I'll skip Paris," you tell Chin Chin. "I figure the security in a king's castle is too hard to penetrate."

South of Paris, not far from the Pyrenees Mountains, the pale stone towers and walls of a medium-sized castle loom into view. Blue-and-gold banners mounted on the topmost towers are whipping in the wind. You activate your stealth shields so you can cruise slowly without being seen.

The castle is well defended from a lofty perch on a rocky cliff high above a river. Just next to it is a small village, and beyond the village, fields and orchards stretch to a dense forest. It's the perfect place to begin your mission.

"Chin Chin, take me down!" you say.

"I figure the best place to land is on one of those turrets, the round towers on the castle wall," he says. "That way you won't have the problem of how to get past those guards outside the door."

"But it might be better to land in the village and get some information first," you tell him. "There are guards patrolling the castle walls, too, and I could get captured while I'm trying to find my way around," you say.

"It's up to you, Inspector," says Chin Chin.

If you decide to land on the castle tower, go on to the next page.

If you choose to land in the village instead, turn to page 29.

Still protected by your stealth shields, you cruise slowly just over the castle wall. When you reach the sixth, and last, tower on the wall, you find what you're looking for—a sleeping guard.

In a flash you've landed. Calling on the power of Turoc, you transform the *Voyager* into a blue-and-gold banner. No one's likely to notice an extra banner streaming from the tower.

Keeping one eye on the sleeping guard, you crouch against the tower wall and take a few deep breaths of the warm Earth atmosphere and move your arms and legs to loosen them up. It takes only a few minutes before you're acclimated to the heavier gravity of Earth.

The Power of Turoc has transformed the jumpsuit you were wearing on board the *Voyager* into a simple loose-fitting tunic. You should be able to pass yourself off as a servant—if you can make it past the heavily guarded castle tower, where servants don't belong!

From your vantage point on top of the tower you notice a rectangular opening. You can see the end of a ladder sticking up through the opening. You tiptoe past the sleeping guard and climb down the ladder to a stone floor about eight feet below. From there, stairs follow the curve of the tower wall, spiraling down forty feet or so to the base of the tower.

You take a deep breath and start down the stairs—but you don't get very far before you run into three guards armed with bows and arrows.

You bow your head meekly and flatten your body against the wall, hoping they'll continue on up the stairs.

The biggest of the three stops in front of you.

"What are you doing up here?" he demands to know. He speaks in a variation of French known only in a small part of Earth. You understand him perfectly, because you are bioformed to understand any language you encounter, but right now you're speechless, unable to imagine what might be the proper answer.

"I'm speaking to you, serf!" the big man says. You know a serf is a servant or worker—almost a slave. Surely these three fellows have something better to do than concern themselves with a lowly serf! But they are looking at you more closely.

"Or *are* you a serf," says one of his companions. "You look too clean to be a serf."

Everyone guffaws at this—though why they're making the strange Earth noises known as laughter is beyond you.

The big fellow—the leader, you suppose—picks up your hand and looks at it.

"You're right, Bernard," he says. "No one with fingernails this clean could possibly be a serf." His face tightens into a scowl. "Only spies have hands this clean!"

"Please," you say. "I mean no harm."

"We'll let Roland be the judge of that!" the big guy says, giving you a jab between the shoulders. "Meanwhile, we're locking you up in the dungeon."

They march you down the spiral staircase, then down some more stairs. These are narrower and steeper, and everything seems to grow darker and danker as you descend. Finally, they throw you into a tiny room. You collapse miserably on the dirt-packed floor. Your first day on Earth isn't going very well.

Go on to the next page.

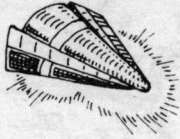

The clanking of chains tells you that you are not alone in the dungeon. By now your eyes have gotten used to the dim light, so you're able to make out a young man sitting a few feet away. His arms are chained to the wall.

The young man—who you later learn is a villager named Henry—seems happy to have someone to talk to. You ask him why he's being punished.

"I got caught hunting rabbits," he tells you. "But I heard I'm going to be released today. They need every hand they can get to bring in the grape harvest."

"What's wrong with hunting rabbits?" you ask.

Henry seems surprised at your ignorance. "Sir Roland's forest is strictly off limits to us villagers— except for certain times when we're allowed to gather wood or look for mushrooms. Hunting is reserved for Roland and his guests."

By now you know that Sir Roland is the young knight who is lord of the castle—along with the village, the fields, and the forest surrounding it. Everyone in the village is expected to do a cer-

tain amount of work for Roland and live by his rules. In exchange he protects them from hostile neighbors.

"How'd he get so much power?" you ask.

"Sir Roland is a fierce fighter," Henry tells you. "The Duke of Aquitaine granted him the castle as a reward."

"And to make sure he stays loyal, I'll bet," you say.

"It works both ways. When you meet Roland, you'll understand why the duke wants him for an ally," says Henry.

"What's this Roland like?" you ask.

"They say he loves a good time almost as much as he loves fighting. He never turns away an entertainer—a singer, a juggler, an acrobat—"

Suddenly you feel a surge of excitement. You remember all those flips and somersaults Simbar made you learn. They just might get you out of the tight spot you're in.

Just then the heavy wooden door to your cell opens, and two guards enter. One of them unchains Henry from the wall.

"Right on time," Henry says with a wink at you as he gets to his feet. You nod good-bye as he's led away. The other guard takes you firmly by the arm and leads you up the dungeon stairs. You recognize him as one of the guards who captured you.

"Where are we going?" you ask.

The guard just glowers at you and tightens his grip on your arm. Once you've climbed up out of the dungeon, he leads you into a vast room. In the middle of the room is a primitive fireplace. Smoke from the fire drifts up to vents in the ceiling high above. A few soot-covered shields decorate the walls. A dozen or so knights and an equal number of sleek-looking dogs lounge around the fire.

At one end of the room, raised on a platform, stands a table. Behind the table sits a stocky young man with restless eyes. He wears a loose tunic, like yours—except his is made of some finer cloth, like velvet. He sits casually, his chin propped on his fist. You assume you're looking at Roland.

"So this is the spy you found cowering on the tower steps!" he says in a fierce voice. His tone is mocking, as though he's challenging the guard to prove his accusation.

The guard takes your hand and thrusts it toward Roland. "Look at these hands! They're not the hands of a serf!"

Roland peers at your palm. "Doesn't mean they're the hands of a spy," he says. Then he looks at you. "Or does it?"

"They are the hands of an acrobat," you say.

"An acrobat!" says Roland, banging his hand on the table. "Well, that's easy enough to prove!"

Roland leans back in his chair and drapes a leg over the side, then motions for you to begin. You move to the middle of the floor. With a flourish, you remove your outer tunic, revealing the costume that Simbar had insisted you wear underneath—a short tunic with flowing sleeves and brightly colored stockings. Then you take a deep breath; you just hope your stuff is good enough for Roland.

You do backflips, frontflips, and even a side-flip—a move you invented yourself. Roland seems to like what he sees, so you end your routine with a handstand right on the table in front of him. Your upside-down face is just inches from his.

Roland pounds on the table some more, looking into your eyes and grinning fiercely.

"You can come down now," he says.

You curl your body into a sumersault that smoothly and gracefully puts you on the floor again.

"You're an acrobat all right!" says Roland.

The guard can see that you're a big hit with Roland. "One of the best I've ever seen," he says. "No wonder we found this prankster in the tower. Only a very skilled acrobat could scale the castle walls!"

"Enough," says Roland. Then he turns to you. "I want you to perform during dinner tonight. And feel free to enjoy the hospitality of my castle."

You bow, feeling relieved, cross the giant room, and enter the sun-filled courtyard outside.

Turn to page 35.

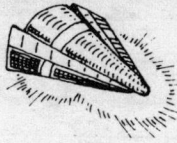

You land in a grove of pines near the edge of the village and transform the *Voyager* into a tree trunk. You pause for a moment and take your first deep breath of warm, fresh Earth air. Then you step out of your hiding place and head into the village.

You walk along a narrow dirt road lined with tiny houses, each with its own small garden. Several people working in gardens nod at you as you pass. You are dressed, as they are, in a loose tunic made of some kind of rough cloth.

When you reach an open area in the center of town, you stop and try to make sense of the scene before you. Men, women, and even children are stomping up and down inside huge wooden vats. Each vat is eight or ten feet in diameter, and three or four feet high. A cart, drawn by a donkey, rumbles up to one of the vats, and the driver dumps what looks like purple grapes into it.

You cautiously approach one of the vats and look inside. A young woman hikes herself up over the edge of the vat, swings her legs over, and wipes purple juice and goo off her feet with the bottom of her tunic. When she sees the startled look on your face, she laughs.

"You'd think you'd never seen anyone crushing grapes before," she says. Fortunately, you are bioformed to understand any Earth language you encounter, even the local variation of French spoken on this part of the planet.

"It's true I've never seen such a thing," you say. "It does seem an odd thing to do."

"I take it you are from far away," she says. "Otherwise you would know that I am doing what we do every year after we harvest the grapes—crushing them to make wine."

You make a mental note not to drink any of the local wine. But the young woman seems friendly, so you manage to hide your feelings as you walk along beside her.

"Some of the wine produced in Aquitaine is the finest in all of France," she tells you.

You know from your Earth studies that Aquitaine is one of the richest areas of France, almost a separate country ruled by a powerful duke named William. Your gaze turns to the castle gates, which you've now reached. William would have granted this castle and its surrounding land to a lesser noble in exchange for his loyalty and support. It could be the home of a count or a knight.

"Who is lord of the castle?" you ask.

"A young knight named Sir Roland," comes the reply. "But I doubt you'll ever see him," she says with a laugh, pointing to the heavily guarded doors.

Just then two people wearing fancy costumes, a man and a woman, approach a castle guard. The woman is plucking on a stringed instrument and dancing, and the man is juggling five brightly colored beanbags. The guard nods, and they are admitted through a small door to one side.

"They say Roland loves to have fun," she tells you. "So the guards are under orders to admit entertainers."

Suddenly you remember the special training you went through for this mission—the handstands, the backflips, the tumbling. Simbar, you're a genius, you think to yourself.

"Then I'll have no trouble meeting Roland," you say. With a flourish, you remove your long brown tunic, revealing brightly colored tights and a belted shirt with flowing sleeves—a costume you had thought a bit odd when Simbar insisted you wear it. Then you hurl your body through a series of flips and twists, ending with an elaborate bow.

The woman claps her hands, delighted by the performance. You wave and turn to the guard, preparing a little speech to persuade him to let you enter the castle, but he's already motioning you through the door.

Turn to page 35.

The castle courtyard you find yourself in is quite large, and very noisy. A cart pulled by a horse rumbles by, loaded with grain. In one corner a blacksmith pulls a piece of white-hot iron out of a fire and lays it on the flat face of a heavy forge. Then you hear the awesome hammering as he shapes the metal into a spear. Armor is being repaired, arrows fitted with steel tips, horses brushed and coddled, and water fetched from a well.

To keep everyone fed, there's a huge kitchen in a building all by itself. You look inside. Eight or ten people are at work. Some are bringing in baskets of food. A boy and a girl are tending meat roasting over a fire in a fireplace so big they could easily stand inside it. There's also an oven big enough to bake dozens of loaves of bread every day.

You marvel at the number and variety of activities it takes to keep a medium-sized castle running smoothly. In fact, the only idle people at the moment are the knights. They do nothing but fight, and since there aren't any battles to be fought at the moment, they spend their time play ing games—chess and some kind of game involving dice.

You're expected to perform for Roland this evening, and you're more than a little nervous about it, so you find a grassy spot and practice. You've just finished going through your moves when you hear someone clapping. It's a sandy-haired boy who looks to be about fifteen. He's looking down at you from his seat astride an enormous horse.

"Not bad," he says. Then he gets down off his horse and sticks out his hand. "I'm Richard."

Richard's body, arms, and legs are covered with what you recognize as chain mail—ingeniously constructed armor made by linking many small steel loops together. The result is a garment tough enough to resist the thrust of a lance or sword, but light and supple enough to allow the wearer to move about fairly easily.

"I take it you're getting ready to go into battle," you say.

Richard laughs. "In a way, yes." He points to a shield hanging from a post about fifty feet away. "I'm practicing for the day when I'll be a knight."

You watch as Richard gallops toward the shield, holding the long pointed weapon Simbar told you about—a lance. Richard's aim is off, so that the shield swings around and a sandbag hits

him in the back. He manages to stay on his horse, however, and trots back to where you're standing.

"It's not an easy thing to learn," he says, rubbing his shoulder.

"I can see that," you reply. You mean to sound sympathetic, but Richard scowls as though he's being taunted.

He leaps off his horse and hands you the reins. "You try it!" he says.

You're startled. But you are being given an opportunity to do something you've been longing to do—ride a real live horse. Trying to remember what you learned on Whirlaway, you swing your body up into the saddle and gather up the reins.

The horse's movements are suprisingly smooth compared with Whirlaway's. It takes only a couple of seconds for you to feel in full command of your mount. Richard hands you his lance, and you trot to the end of the field. Then you urge your horse into a gallop.

It's a thrilling ride—but it's all over in about ten seconds. Your lance barely grazes its target, and when the sandbag swings around, it knocks you out of the saddle.

Your body slams onto the ground so hard you see stars. It takes a while to get to your feet. By the time you do, Richard has chased down his horse, retrieved his lance, and is standing by your side looking worried.

He's surprised when you say, "Let me try again."

Earth Inspectors are supplied with superb Earthling bodies—strong, well coordinated, and resilient—so they're able to acquire new skills very rapidly. You're almost sure that your second try will be successful.

Once again, you climb into the saddle and gallop toward your target, steadying the lance against your body. But this time, your lance finds its mark on the shield.

Richard looks at you, puzzled. "How'd you learn so fast?"

You shrug modestly.

It works.

Richard smiles at you. You've made a friend.

Go on to the next page.

It's always good to have a friendly Earthling to talk to, so you spend the rest of the afternoon with Richard. You learn that this knight-in-training was sent to the castle by his parents when he was only seven years old. He started his training as a page, running errands, and then last year, when he was fourteen, he moved up a notch to squire. He's very proud that he's Roland's personal squire.

"What do you do?" you ask him.

"Anything Roland asks me to," says Richard. "I clean his armor, take care of his horse, help him dress for battle, wait on him at dinner—"

Richard then tells you that a great banquet is planned for that evening, in honor of William, the duke of Aquitaine.

"Just where is Aquitaine?" you ask.

The look on Richard's face tells you that you've asked another dumb question. If you hadn't been so impressive with the lance, he probably wouldn't bother answering, but instead he shrugs and makes a wide gesture with his arms.

"You're right in the middle of it," he says. "Covers almost all of southwest France—from the

Loire River to the Pyrenees Mountains. William's duchy is the largest one in France—and the richest."

You feel a few nervous flutters in your stomach when you hear you'll be performing for the most powerful duke in France!

Turn to page 43.

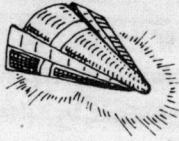

A few hours later, you enter the great hall of the castle. The floor is strewn with flowers. Light from candles, torches, and a huge fireplace casts a golden glow over the dinner in progress. There must be sixty men and women seated at long tables. Squires and servants—among them your new friend, Richard—rush about with platters of food. At the other end of the room you see Roland presiding over the dinner from a table raised on a platform. A huge man next to Roland is the center of attention. It must be William.

The whole scene reminds you of an elegant circus. A man and a woman are juggling wooden clubs, a magician is entertaining some of the diners with magic tricks, and three musicians up on a balcony play music for everyone. It's all very casual, so when Roland motions to you to begin your performance, you hardly feel nervous at all.

Maybe that's why it all goes so smoothly. Roland and his guests at the head table seem so delighted by your flips and handstands that you decide to try something even more spectacular. Quickly you set up a long plank so it's supported by two of the dining tables. Then you perform more handstands and flips on this improvised balance beam, ending with a series of backflips and

44

a triple somersault onto the ground. You nail your landing so solidly that they practically have to pry you from the floor—and you've managed to end up right in front of Roland and his guest of honor.

"A wonderful performance!" proclaims Roland. He makes room for you at the table, squeezing you in between the duke and the duke's daughter, Eleanor. Duke William is in the middle of a long story involving a battle he and Roland fought together, so you turn your attention to his daughter.

Eleanor—a tall, dazzling blonde wearing a long silk dress and flashy gold jewelry—compliments you on your performance. She is so poised and elegant, you're surprised when you later learn that she's only fourteen years old.

"What brings you to Roland's castle?" you ask.

"Father travels around Aquitaine a lot," she says. "I often go with him." She leans closer and whispers, "I think he'd go mad if he had to stay in one place—and so would I."

You can't believe your luck! You're sitting right next to someone who's seen more castles than almost any other Earthling you could hope to meet.

You look intensely into Eleanor's big blue eyes. "Is it possible that a city would have to be built to capture one of these castles?"

Eleanor looks thoughtful. "I suppose if a castle were very, very big—" She picks up her chalice, sips, then puts it down again. "But there aren't any castles that big. In Aquitaine, or anyplace else."

Eleanor has just supplied you with an important clue. In fact, you have enough information to move your mission to another time frame. But there's no way to leave just now, so you relax and enjoy the rest of the entertainment.

Several knights, known as troubadours, sing and play a stringed instrument called a lute. The songs mostly have to do with a knight who falls madly in love with a woman, and how difficult it is to win her, but how they'll keep trying no matter how long it takes. The knights all look at Eleanor while they sing. You make a mental note to find out later who it is she's going to end up with.

Watching Eleanor and the others enjoying themselves, you can see that Earthlings love to have fun just as much as Turonians.

At the same time, the banquets and games, the entertainment and music, are forming William's knights and Roland's knights into a tightly knit— and loyal—group. A very useful thing to be part of, when any day you could find yourself having to defend against attackers!

When the party's about over, you say goodnight to Eleanor, shake hands with Roland and William, and slip out of the great hall.

Within an hour, you're back on board the *Voyager*. You decide to go into orbit around the Earth so you can plan your next move.

Turn to page 84.

You wait until the castle's inhabitants have settled down for the night. Guards armed with crossbows and heavy guns are stationed in the towers and along the outer walls, but they're looking out toward the enemy camp. It's easy to land in one of the inner courtyards without being seen. You pick a spot next to a fountain made of stone lions supporting a huge basin. Soon you're on the ground.

You step out onto the smooth marble surface of the courtyard and transform your spacecraft into a stone turtle. You're about to place it in the waters of the fountain when you hear footsteps approaching. You just have time to duck into the shadowy recesses of a small nook.

You're trapped. All you can do is crouch against the wall and hope whoever's coming won't find you.

A man and a woman enter the courtyard and stop near the fountain. The man is wearing a long, loose robe made of some kind of rich fabric. On his head is a turban. The woman is also dressed in silky fabrics. Golden bracelets glitter from her arms and ankles. She is sobbing quietly.

"You must listen to me, Boabdil," she says.

Boabdil! You realize you're looking at the king of Granada himself, Boabdil el Chico—the Unlucky!

El Chico shakes his head. "We have no choice. Our people are beginning to starve. *And* our horses. The king of Spain has cut off our food supplies and burned almost all our fields. Now my spies tell me he intends to burn the only gardens left—the ones just outside the city walls. We *have* to fight."

"But think of our son and our daughter," the woman cries. "If we lose, I can't bear to think what will happen to them."

El Chico sighs. "I have thought of surrender. But the people don't want it. Not yet, at least."

El Chico and his wife disappear through an arched doorway, leaving you to think about what you've just heard. If there's going to be a battle, you'd better find a safer place to hide.

You look up at the stars. You can tell by their position in the sky that there isn't much left of the night. Then you notice the stone turtle in your hand. Of course, you could get out of here. You might be better off in the Spanish camp.

If you decide to stay in the Alhambra, go on to the next page.

If you choose to leave, turn to page 57.

It's easy to see why El Chico doesn't want to give up his home, you think as you make a moon-lit tour in search of a hiding place. The Alhambra must be the most delightful castle in Europe. The rooms are hung with silk, and there are gardens, fountains, and pools everywhere. You find a good hiding place—a small room off a courtyard near the stables. A couple of big silk-covered pillows make a comfortable bed, and it isn't long before you fall asleep, lulled by the sound of water splashing in a nearby fountain, and the smell of orange blossoms.

Early the next morning you're startled awake by the sound of blaring trumpets—the call to battle!

Looking out from your hiding place, you can see a parade of magnificent horses go by. The horses' heads are protected with armor, and they wear colorful fittings of green-and-crimson velvet trimmed with silver and gold. Each horse is be-ing led by a young groom. You follow the parade to a courtyard where men are being dressed in armor decorated with more gold and silver.

Another blare of trumpet music announces the arrival of Boabdil. He's going into battle in the fan-

ciest armor of all—and with a jeweled saddle for his pure white horse. He greets his magnificent, half-starved knights. Then, in a flourish of trumpets and waving banners, hoofbeats and hurrahs, they all gallop off to meet the enemy.

You and everyone else crowd onto the castle towers to watch the battle below.

Through the din and dirt you can barely make out what's happening. Swords clash. Arrows fly. Horses fall to the ground. Knights are pushed off their mounts where they can only lie helplessly.

The Spanish knights and their horses—as splendid-looking as their Moorish foes—seem to be getting the worst of it, but the Moorish foot soldiers suddenly panic and turn back. The guns firing from the castle walls keep the Spanish knights at a distance, but by the time they head back to their camp, the Spanish have accomplished their mission: The last of the gardens and orchards are going up in smoke.

What's left of the Moors straggle back. A gloom settles over the castle. With food supplies critically low, it's only a matter of time until its inhabitants will be starved into submission.

You notice a knight riding toward you on a gray horse. When he gets to where you're standing, you can see that he must be in trouble—he's barely able to hold himself in the saddle and the reins are flapping loosely on the horse's neck. As

he passes close to you, he topples over and falls to the ground. Quickly you raise the face plate on his helmet. His young face is flushed from heat.

"Water," he gasps.

You get water from a nearby fountain. Then you help the knight out of his armor. He has several scars on his arms and legs—souvenirs of past battles.

"Thank you, friend," says the knight, who you later learn is named Assad. "I would have died of the heat if you hadn't helped me."

Go on to the next page.

For the next forty-eight hours you and Assad work side by side, doing what you can to help the wounded, exhausted soldiers. When you're finally able to get some sleep, you're awakened by excited shouts. Everyone is looking toward a bright glow where the Spanish are camped. Incredible as it seems, the whole place is going up in flames!

Assad claps you on the back. "Surely the Spaniards will have to give up their siege now," he says.

But the next morning, the Spanish army seems to rise from the ashes of the camp. Trumpets sound. Horses and knights prance around in their finery as though they had something to celebrate.

No one knows what to make of this strange behavior. "But it's clear the Spanish are not leaving in defeat," says Assad with a sigh.

Even more stunnning surprises are to come: In a matter of weeks, an entire city is built outside the Alhambra. "I can't believe it," says Assad as he watches sturdy buildings, powerful walls, and tall towers rising. Right in the middle of the city is a huge square "big enough to hold the entire Spanish army," as Assad puts it.

Then you, Assad, and all the other hungry people locked inside the castle watch as long trains of pack mules arrive in the new city, laden with food. Merchants open up shops to sell all the luxuries Spanish lords and ladies can't do without.

It's a brilliant tactic—the Moors are so disheartened by this show of Spanish strength and determination, surely they will surrender soon.

You realize you've found the city you've been seeking for so long! Now you must try to find your fellow Earth Inspector, Teega. You wait until dark, then you transform the stone turtle back into your spacecraft and head for the city. Once on board, you down an Orange Phyzz, feeling a bit guilty that you're unable to share it with your hungry friend Assad.

You land inside the city, in a quiet spot near a freshly built church, and transform the *Voyager* into a boulder. Then you go inside and stretch out on one of the brand-new church pews. You haven't slept in days, and you have a feeling you'll need your wits about you to cope with what lies ahead.

Turn to page 94.

Moments later, your *Voyager* spacecraft is flying over the Spanish camp. Down below, you see rows of small tents and huts made of the branches of trees. There's a stable for horses, and a deep trench to keep out intruders.

One area has larger, more luxurious tents. You pick a landing spot near the largest tent of all.

In an instant you're on the ground, transforming your spacecraft into a boulder.

You've landed next to what must rate as the most dazzling tent on Earth. It's bigger than most well-off Earthlings' houses, and it's covered with colorful decorations. You're wondering what the inside is like when you see a young boy kneeling down next to the side of the tent. He picks up the side of a tent flap. Then he looks around quickly. When he sees you watching him, a look of terror crosses his face.

"Please don't tell anyone you saw me," he says in a terrified whisper. "I only wanted to see what it's like in the queen's tent."

"The queen's tent?" you say. "What would a queen be doing camping out with an army?"

The boy looks slightly less terrified. "I'll tell you anything you want to know if you promise not to report me," he says in a whisper.

"It's a deal," you say. Maybe you've gotten lucky. This kid may be just the right person to tell you everything you need to know.

"You're a spy for the enemy, aren't you?" he says.

"I'm just a curious stranger—like you," you say with a tiny smile.

The boy seems to accept this explanation for your presence. He sticks out his hand. "My name is Pedro."

You're about to tell him your name when a very loud trumpet fanfare sounds. The two of you look down a muddy lane to see a procession nearing the tent. You can make out armored knights on armored horses, brightly uniformed attendants bearing colorful banners—and Queen Isabella herself!

Turn to page 60.

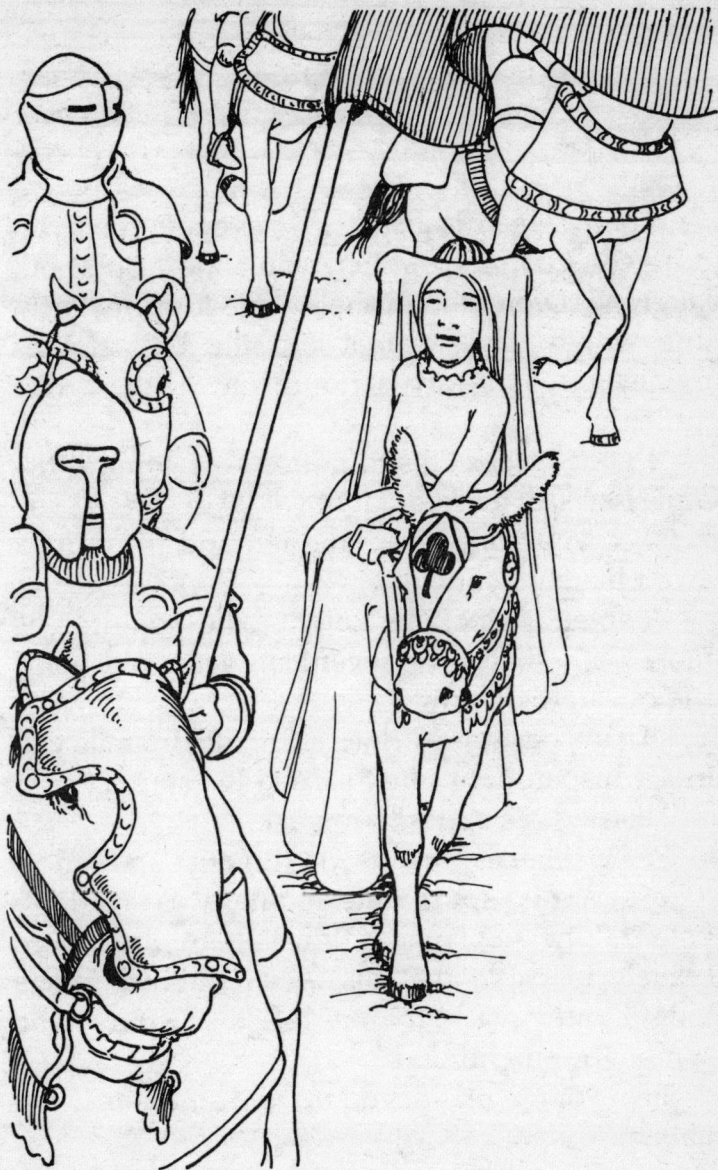

When Queen Isabella is close enough so you can get a good look at her, you almost burst out laughing. Even though she's a fine-looking Earthling with noble features and the best clothes money can buy, she's riding on a little white mule!

No one else seems to notice how comical the mule looks all decked out in wildly decorated velvets, so you stifle your laughter and try to look awed like everyone else.

A splendid-looking knight who couldn't be more than sixteen or seventeen years old helps the queen dismount.

"That's her son—Prince Juan," Pedro tells you in a whisper. "He's just earned his spurs."

"Earned his spurs?" you ask.

Pedro shakes his head at your ignorance. "'Earned his spurs' means he was made a knight," he explains. "Prince Juan fought so bravely in battle that his father dubbed him a knight and gave him a pair of silver spurs—the symbol of knighthood."

Two young girls dismount and stand near the queen.

"Those are the princesses," Pedro informs you.

The queen, Prince Juan, and the princesses disappear inside the tent, followed by dozens of attendants and guards. Behind them are twenty or thirty mules with big packs strapped on their backs. They must be carrying the queen's luggage. You're beginning to see why she needs a roomy place.

The mule train is led forward, and servants rush over to remove the packs. You grab Pedro by the arm and steer him toward one of the mules. "This is how we're going to get inside the queen's tent!" you tell him.

Go on to the next page.

Minutes later, struggling under the burden of a heavy, lumpy pack, you and Pedro enter the tent. You just have time to take in the shimmering interior, hung with silken fabrics and furnished with fancy carpets and furniture, before a stern-looking guard escorts you back outside.

The queen's kitchen help is distributing food to the servants, so you and Pedro help yourselves to some bread and meat and find an out-of-the-way place to sit and talk.

"You still haven't answered my question," you say. "What is the queen doing in the middle of an army camp?"

"It's part of a very smart plan," says your new friend as he bites into a hunk of meat. "Queen Isabella and King Ferdinand don't really want to have to go into battle for the Alhambra. They're hoping to make a show of force so the enemy will lose heart."

Not a bad tactic, you think as you gaze at the mighty castle in the distance. "I suppose to the people cooped up inside the Alhambra, it looks as though this place is one nonstop festival. They must be wondering how they're going to be able to hold out."

"You bet they are," says Pedro. "They're completely cut off from their supplies. And the Spanish king has seen to it that most of their fields and orchards are destroyed." He finishes off the last of his bread. "Come on, let's find a place to sleep. There's a rumor going 'round that there's going to be some action tomorrow.

It's a warm night, so you fall asleep under the stars.

Go on to the next page.

The next morning you're awakened by the sound of trumpets and drums. The knights assemble on their horses, surrounded by foot soldiers, and move off across the plain.

Pedro's not about to miss the action, and he doesn't have much difficulty persuading you to join him, so the two of you borrow a couple of horses from the stable and follow along behind the army.

Once again, you silently thank Simbar for seeing to it that you're trained to ride a horse. What would Pedro think if you told him you'd learned to ride on another planet!

Unfortunately, Pedro isn't much of a horseman. When the battle gets under way, his horse gets so upset by the noise that he throws Pedro to the ground and gallops off back toward camp.

"Are you hurt?" you ask Pedro as you dust him off and help him to his feet.

"Just a little dizzy," he says.

"Let's skip the battle," you suggest. "Maybe they'll have another one tomorrow."

You pull Pedro up behind your saddle and return to camp. Some time later, the knights and foot soldiers follow. From what you gather, the day has been a triumph. The last of the orchards and fields have been torched, drastically reducing the food supplies of the Moors.

"It won't be long before they'll have to give up their castle," Pedro tells you.

Go on to the next page.

But two days later, a disaster strikes the Spanish camp.

You're about to fall asleep when you notice the smell of smoke in the air. "Pedro, wake up!" you say, jabbing him in the side.

The two of you scramble to your feet. Off in the distance you see a great orange ball of fire.

"It's the queen's tent!" says Pedro.

You watch helplessly as the fire spreads through the tents and makeshift huts. There's nothing anyone can do, and by morning the entire camp has gone up in flames.

"The Moors must be responsible for this!" says Pedro. But soon the word is out. It's no conspiracy. The fire was an accident, caused by one of the queen's attendants when she set a candle too close to a curtain.

Go on to the next page.

The next morning, you're astonished to see the king and queen up bright and early. Trumpets sound. Drums roll. Knights in armor parade. It's as though nothing has happened!

"What's going on?" you wonder aloud.

Pedro supplies an answer. "You have to hand it to Ferdinand and Isabella. They know they're being watched. They want the enemy to think everything's under control."

And everything *is* under control, as it turns out. It isn't long before Ferdinand and Isabella have a stunning piece of news. Instead of just bringing in new tents for everyone, they intend to build an entire city!

With astonishing speed, the city rises—walls, towers, squares, and huge buildings. In a matter of weeks, it's finished. Some people want to name it after Queen Isabella, but it's named Santafé instead.

You observe the construction with growing excitement, knowing it's the city you're been looking for. "But why would they build an entire city?" you ask Pedro one day.

"It's purely for show," he says. Then he points to the Alhambra off in the distance. "Just imagine how they feel, locked up inside there. They know they can't stand up against an enemy with this much power."

Pedro is right. It isn't long before the king of the Moors, known as Boabdil the Unlucky, sends a message to the Spanish rulers. He's ready to surrender.

Part of your mission is complete. But now, you must find your fellow Earth Inspector, Teega—and see if you can save her life.

Turn to page 94.

In less than an hour, you're on board the *Voyager*, streaking through the dark side of the Earth's sky. You just have time to pick out your home planet's sun—the bright star called Bellatrix in the constellation of Orion—before you feel the *Voyager* break free from Earth's gravity.

You're now entering the space–time continuum. It's an 800-trillion-mile trip back to Turoc, but you experience this enormous journey as a whisper of time.

When you arrive, Simbar himself is there to greet you.

"I am very glad you are safe," he says. "When Teega returned to Turoc, I knew you had succeeded in your mission—but I began to fear you had sacrificed your life for her." He cranes his neck back to look up at you. "I can tell by the smile on your Earthling face that you are feeling well."

"Indeed I am," you say. "I am eager to tell you about my adventures!"

"And I am eager to listen," says Simbar.

Just then a jet rover swoops down and buzzes by just over your head. It's Shala and Zy! Through the window of the cockpit you can see them giving you an Earthling sign of approval—the thumbs-up sign. You're a little surprised to see that your skyboard is stuck in the back of the jet rover.

"Before we discuss your latest Earth findings, I have another mission for you," Simbar says, after the jet rover has finished its flyby.

You try to look enthusiastic. You'd been looking forward to spending some time with your friends. "And what is the new mission?" you ask.

Simbar's great eyes twinkle. "I'm ordering you to the Sea of Turoc with Shala and Zy for three days of skyboarding."

You feel a surge of joy. "Thanks, Simbar," you say. "I'd like to return to planet Earth, and soon. But right now, three days in the surf sounds just perfect!"

The End

"Get me to the year 2000," you tell Chin Chin once you're in the air.

"But, Inspector, hardly any Earthlings live in castles in the year 2000," Chin Chin says. "And no one would capture a castle by building a city. Earthlings are equipped with such powerful weapons it wouldn't be necessary."

"True," you say. "But with all due respect, Chin Chin, there are a lot of gaps in the historical data you have stored in your memory. For instance, you didn't warn me that when I landed in the year 1349 I'd find myself right in the middle of the Black Death!"

"What's that?" Chin Chin asks.

"An epidemic that wiped out one-third of the people on Earth!" you tell him.

"Sorry, Inspector," says Chin Chin. "And I hope you're feeling all right."

You haven't been able to stop yourself from constantly checking your armpits for lumps and your skin for black splotches. So far, so good. You pop open a bottle of Orange Phyzz. All you can do is keep yourself in top condition and hope for the best.

72

"I still fail to see why you intend to visit Earth in the year 2000," Chin Chin says.

"I'm going to do some research," you answer.

"Where do you want to go, then?" he asks.

"Let's try Zurich, in Switzerland."

"Why there?"

"It's a big city. It's got to have a good university."

"Anything you say, Inspector," says Chin Chin as he sets his coordinates.

Go on to the next page.

Looking out from the cockpit, you see a very different Europe loom into view. Cities with tall skyscrapers, airports, superhighways—things none of the Earthlings you've met so far on your mission would have ever even dreamed of.

"Europe in the year 2000 functions like one nation in some ways," Chin Chin tells you. "In 1992 the European Common Market eliminated a lot of red tape that made it difficult for someone in, say, France, to do business with someone in Italy or Spain. A united Europe can compete like other big economic powers—the United States and Japan, for instance."

As your spacecraft nears Zurich, you catch sight of the highest mountains in Europe—the Alps. The snow-covered mountains are a beautiful sight, but as your spacecraft drops down closer to Earth, the landscape suddenly disappears. You're in the midst of a blizzard!

"Chin Chin! Abort the landing!" you say.

"I didn't see the storm coming," says Chin Chin. You wait anxiously as he makes some whirring noises. "In fact, I don't know where we are right now. Something's happened to my scanner."

It couldn't have come at a worse time. You can't see a thing, and without the scanner, Chin

Chin is useless. You'll just have to take the controls and try to steer back up through the storm without crashing into a mountain.

Suddenly the snow squall stops. You're heading straight for a wall of rock!

You jerk the controls to the right. The *Voyager* responds, going into a roll, then a dive as it veers away from disaster. You level off and find a gap between two rocky peaks. It's just big enough for your spacecraft, but you're an excellent pilot so you have no trouble making it through.

Once you're through the gap, the landscape opens up enough so you're able to find a level place to land near a tiny village. You're probably nowhere near Zurich. You notice cable cars transporting people to the top of the mountain. You've landed in the midst of a ski resort.

You can't transform your spacecraft because Chin Chin needs to get to work on the scanner problem.

"I'm programmed to go through my data bank and find the problem, then fix it myself. But it'll take a while," he tells you.

There's nothing you can do. Oh, well. You've always wanted to try skiing. You bury the *Voyager* under a mound of snow and lay a big rock on top so you'll be able to find it. Then you put on your warmest clothes, sling a pack on your back, and head for the village.

Go on to the next page.

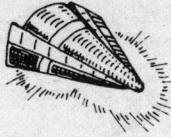

An hour later you've rented a pair of skis and you're riding the chair lift up a slope of the mountain. Sitting beside you is the instructor you've hired to get you started skiing downhill. His name is Spencer, and his skis look twice as long as yours—the sure sign of an expert, you've learned.

"I'm an American," he tells you, after you ask him about his accent. "Skied for the University of Colorado from 'eighty-eight to 'ninety-one. Came here to Switzerland for a ski vacation and decided to stay. I was lucky to get this job." He sees you've arrived at the top of the ski lift. "Time to get off," he says.

Spencer shows you how to curl your body forward slightly so you can ski away from the chair lift. Then the two of you stand for a moment to take in the scene. The sky is a brilliant blue. The snow is powdery and soft. And dozens of skiers, dressed in the latest brightly colored ski clothes, are zooming down the hill.

Spencer is an excellent instructor, and it isn't long before he has you making a graceful curving path down a gentle slope.

"Are you sure you're a beginner?" he asks. "I don't think I've ever seen anyone make as rapid progress as you are!"

You wish you could tell Spencer the truth—that Earth Inspectors are equipped with a superb synthetic Earthling body, capable of learning new skills more rapidly than most Earthlings. But you can't. It's against the code.

You glide to a halt when you've reached bottom.

"You're something else—you're already advanced enough for a much more challenging trail," Spencer tells you.

Motioning for you to follow, he leads the way to another chair lift.

As you let the chair lift scoop you up, he turns his dazzling smile on you. "We're going to the top this time," he says. "It'll take a while, so you might as well relax."

"What did you study at the University of Colorado?" you ask once you're under way.

"I majored in history," he says. "My specialty was Western Europe."

You can't believe your luck. "Then you must know about the fighting that went on over castles," you say.

" You're talking about the feudal period—the Middle Ages," he says. "Back then, the castle was the main line of defense. But the problem was that the castles became impossible to attack. They just didn't have the weapons. So the only way to take a castle was to surround it and cut off the food supplies—starve the inhabitants into submission."

"In one case, they built a city to capture a castle," you say.

Spencer nods thoughtfully and looks off into the snowy distance. You're so eager to hear what he's going to say next that you're afraid it shows.

"Umm, yes," he finally says. "That would be the siege of Granada—when the king and queen of Spain finally succeeded in throwing out the Moors."

"The Moors? Who were they?" you ask.

"The Moors were people who came from North Africa—from what's now Morocco. They loved Spain, and they built some fabulous castles and mosques."

"Mosques?" you ask.

"Mosques were religious centers," Spencer tells you. "The Moors practiced a religion called Islam. They'd been in Spain for almost eight hundred years by the time King Ferdinand and Queen Isabella launched their siege on Granada."

"Why did they want the Moors out?" you ask.

"At that time, the Spanish had no tolerance for any other religion except their own—Christianity. Everyone else, all the outsiders like the Moors, had to go." Spencer gives you a sly smile. "Of course, the Spanish were getting a beautiful hunk of land and all those castles at the same time."

"Tell me about the last siege," you say eagerly.

"It must have been something. Things started to come to a head in the summer of 1491. The king and his troops were there. Then Isabella arrived with her children and servants. They wanted King Boabdil to know they meant business."

"Boabdil?"

"Boabdil the Unlucky, they called him," says Spencer. "He was the last king of the Moors in Spain. There he was, holed up in the most beautiful castle in the world. It was called the Alhambra."

You've arrived at the top of the mountain by now. It's so much fun skiing with Spencer that you decide to wait until later to ask him more questions.

"This time, just follow me," he tells you.

You follow Spencer down a much steeper slope than the one you've just been on, trying to imitate the easy way he uses his body and legs. It's an exhilarating run down the mountain. By the time you reach bottom, you're even able to jump over snowbanks.

This time, when you glide to a halt, the lifts are closed. You have a lot more questions for Spencer, but you have a funny feeling you should check on Chin Chin's progress with the scanner. So you arrange to meet Spencer later that night.

Go on to the next page.

It's a good thing you decided to check on Chin
Chin. When you get close enough to where you'd
buried the *Voyager*, you can see its sleek metal hull
sticking out of the snow. Maybe the heat from the
spaceship melted the snow, or maybe the wind blew
it off. Whatever happened, you hope you're in time
to keep your craft from being discovered! You clear
away more snow and settle into the cockpit.

"Chin Chin," you say, "what's the status of
the scanner?"

"I've found the problem, Inspector," is his reply. "Now all I have to do is fix it."

From where you're sitting in the cockpit you
can see a couple of kids pointing toward the *Voyager*. You've been spotted! You activate the engines. "We can't wait," you tell Chin Chin.
"We've got to take off. Now!"

The kids are running toward you by now, yell-
ing excitedly to each other. You press the throt-
tle forward, and minutes later you're streaking
through the starry sky, traveling faster than any
human eye can follow you. You wonder what the
kids will think when the sleek metal object
they've spotted seems magically to just disappear.

Go on to the next page.

Once you're airborne, you locate Granada on the map of Spain and set a course for the summer of 1491.

You're traveling over France when Chin Chin stops whirring.

"I've fixed the scanner," he reports in triumph. "So I'm able to take over the controls now."

"It's okay, Chin Chin," you say. "I'm having a great time. Don't get enough of this flying stuff now that they've invented you."

Soon the walled city of Granada comes into view. Looming over the city, surrounded by still more walls, is an enormous castle. It has to be the one Spencer told you about—the Alhambra. You activate stealth so you can cruise slowly over the castle. It's an awesome sight: You count thirteen towers in the thick castle walls. Inside, you see beautiful gardens and patios, and water everywhere, in fountains, in pools, cascading in waterfalls.

But no one is strolling in the gardens or enjoying the pools. They're nervously checking their weapons and their armor—no doubt hoping they'll be ready to defend their castle. You're tempted to land inside the castle walls.

Several miles in the distance you can make out the tents of an army camp. If Spencer is right, the king and queen of Spain are there, along with their glittering attendants.

As for Teega, she could be either place. It's hard to decide where to land.

If you decide to land inside the walls of the Alhambra, turn to page 46.

If you'd rather land in the Spanish army camp, turn to page 57.

As soon as the *Voyager* settles into orbit around Earth, you turn to Chin Chin.

"Do you have anything on Eleanor, the daughter of the Duke of Aquitaine?"

You hear the metallic hum that means Chin Chin is searching his databank.

"Here's something," he says after a few seconds. "Not long after you met her, Eleanor's father died and she was married to the king of France."

"You mean Louis the Fat?" you ask. The thought of Eleanor being married off to some fat king makes you shudder.

"No. She married his son, the future king, also named Louis," Chin Chin tells you.

"But she was only fourteen years old!" you say.

"She'd just turned fifteen, actually. Louis was just sixteen," says Chin Chin. "Don't forget, she'd just inherited a huge area in France. The marriage was arranged so that the king could gain control of it."

Chin Chin is humming again. "Listen to this, Inspector," he says after he stops. "Her marriage to King Louis ended badly. But almost immediately, she married the king of England."

"How could that happen?" you ask.

"Sorry, that's all I have," is the reply.

Someday you'd like to solve that riddle. But right now, you must continue your search for the city built to capture a castle.

You lean back in the pilot's seat, bite into a Nutrimax bar, and try to think what to do.

Suddenly, you realize you've been ignoring an important clue: the suit of armor Teega was wearing when she returned from her ill-fated mission. It was nothing like the armor Roland and his knights were wearing. Instead of chain mail, it was made of heavy solid steel plates. Your mind races along. Heavy, cumbersome armor. Why would anyone wear something so impractical?

The answer comes in a flash: to protect against more lethal weapons than Roland and his knights were dealing with. That means Teega had to have been on Earth at a much later date.

Quickly you activate your computron: "Chin Chin, I want to move ahead in time a couple of hundred years. Let's land in, say, 1349."

"Any particular place, Inspector?"

"We'll decide that when we get to Europe," you answer.

Go on to the next page.

You enter the space–time continuum. It always produces a pleasant sensation of being relaxed, focused, and just a little giddy all at once. Even though you're traveling faster than the speed of light, you feel as if you're floating toward your destination.

Two hundred and thirteen Earth years later, Chin Chin sends a tiny electrical shock through your body. You've arrived.

You're eager to find out how Europe has changed. But when you look through the port-hole of your spacecraft, you're hardly prepared for what you see!

Sure, there are more castles, and bigger towns. That doesn't surprise you. But something about the landscape gives you an uneasy feeling. Fields look overgrown and weedy. The trees in the orchards look neglected. And too many villages look like ghost towns, devoid of life. Instead of bright banners, you see black flags flying from their towers.

"Chin Chin, what's going on?" you ask.

"There's a war on," he tells you. "The English and the French have been fighting for ten years.

And they have another ninety years to go before the Hundred Years' War is over."

"But we've just flown over Italy. And now we're over Germany. They look just as bad."

"Sorry, I don't know why things look the way they do," Chin Chin tells you. "I've scanned all the data I have on wars during this period."

Something is definitely wrong with planet Earth. You'd like to find out what it is, but it might be very risky.

It might be wiser to land in a later time frame, you think.

If you decide to land and find out what's wrong, go on to the next page.

If you think it's wiser to land in a later time frame, turn to page 105.

You experience a feeling of dread as you direct Chin Chin to land in an overgrown field near a good-sized town. Checking your map of Germany, you see that the town is named Bremen. Something tells you to bring along provisions, so you put some Nutrimax bars and several bottles of Orange Phyzz in a knapsack. You also stuff in a couple of extra tunics like the one you're wearing.

You step out into knee-deep weeds and transform your spaceship into a broken fence post. You decide to head for Bremen, setting out over the lifeless landscape. Off in the distance you see some strange brown lumps. A few minutes of walking and you're close enough to make out what they are. Cows. Dead cows. There must be thirty of them.

With a growing sense of alarm you continue on toward the city. Stumbling across the rutted field toward you are two children. You're even more alarmed when they're close enough for you to get a clear look at them. The children, both of whom look to be about ten years old, seem dazed. Their clothes—fancy gold-trimmed outfits of silk and velvet—are torn, dirty, and ragged.

The girl speaks through parched lips. "Please—we are so thirsty," she whispers.

You quickly remove two bottles of Orange Phyzz from your knapsack and pop them open.

The children drink eagerly. They're so desperate to get some liquid into themselves that they just stand there in the middle of the field and drink until the bottles are empty.

They seem much revived after they've finished. Of course you can't tell them, but they've just downed eight ounces of the favorite, and most nutritious, drink ever created on the planet Turoc. No food or liquid on Earth contains nearly as much potent nourishment.

"Thank you," says the boy, shaking your hand. "I am Hans. This is my twin sister, Heidi."

"Where are you two headed?" you ask.

Heidi brushes a lock of dirty brown hair off her face. "We don't know. We're looking for food." She looks vaguely back over her shoulder toward Bremen. "There's nothing left there."

"But what has happened?" you ask.

"A horrible disease has descended on us," says Hans. He takes his sister's hand. "It started around Christmas. Everyone is dying." A tear rolls down his cheek. He wipes it away angrily. "Our sister and brother died. Then our mother. Then, two days ago, our father."

"Isn't there anyone who can help you?"

"You are the first person we have seen who is not sick. Or busy trying to help the people who are," Hans tells you. "So many people are dying so fast, there's nothing to do with the bodies but dump them in the street. There's no one to bury them."

It seems to help the children to talk. Now Heidi breaks in: "It happens so quickly! First there's a swelling in the armpit the size of an egg. Then huge sores appear, and black splotches all over. Then comes sweating, and coughing up blood—and then it's all over."

With growing alarm, you realize Heidi is describing a terrible calamity you'd learned about in an Earth studies course back on Turoc—the Bubonic Plague.

Go on to the next page.

The plague, also known as the Black Death, had spread fast, killing people and animals, and even wiping out entire villages. Bremen, the city off in the distance, had been hard hit. Two-thirds of the people living there had died.

You look at the two children in front of you. It's a miracle they're still alive. If only you could whisk them aboard the *Voyager* and drop them off in another century! But that would be interfering in the history of another planet—something Earth Inspectors are strictly forbidden to do.

As it gets dark, Hans points to a stone structure. "We could stay there tonight," he says.

The structure is a deserted barn. You make Hans and Heidi wait outside while you inspect it.

Inside you see why the building is deserted. Everything but the stone walls and some of the wooden roof has been destroyed in a recent fire.

Quickly, a plan forms in your head. No one on Earth knows what you do about the plague—that it was carried by fleas and rats. The recent fire in the barn should have taken care of the fleas and rats. You just hope you can get Hans and Heidi to follow your instructions.

"I can't stay with you," you tell them. "But I can help you survive."

First, the three of you gather wood and build a fire. Then, hoping that the water isn't polluted, you have them bathe in a nearby stream and put on the extra tunics you brought along. Meanwhile, you burn their clothes. It's only then that you allow them to enter the barn.

"Don't go near any people or animals," you tell them. "And keep the fire going." You dump the Nutrimax bars and the bottles of Orange Phyzz out of your knapsack. "These will keep you going for a while." The twins are hearty enough to have survived living in a plague-ridden house. They may even have developed an immunity so they won't get sick. You're hoping the superpotent food supplies you're giving them will build them up so they can survive until the plague ends. From the sound of things, the disease should have run its course in a few weeks.

You give each of them a good-bye hug. "You're going through the worst disaster Earth has ever known," you tell them gravely. "But I know you can make it. And life will get better."

"Don't worry," says Heidi. "Hans and I will do as you say." And for the first time, she smiles.

You return to the broken fence post, transform it back into your spacecraft, and give the command: "Transit."

Turn to page 71.

Early the next morning you begin your search for Teega. Everyone in the city—King Ferdinand and Queen Isabella, the royal children, knights, squires, archers, servants, and you—is heading for a huge square in the center of the city. You wonder if you're about to witness King Boabdil's surrender.

The knights on their horses are a magnificent sight—they're in full armor, with plumes on their helmets flying in the wind. You have an uneasy feeling that hidden inside one of those suits of armor is the Earth Inspector you're looking for. It would be just like Teega to find a movable hiding place, even though she's risking plenty! But how can you possibly identify her in this mass of metal bodies?

A blast of trumpet music interrupts your thoughts. Then a party of Moorish knights rides through the city gates. Through the crowd you see them dismount. One of them has a small boy by the hand. He leads the child to the king and queen. You're not sure, but you think the child is crying.

"What's going on?" you ask a young woman standing next to you.

"They're handing over King Boabdil's son as hostage," she explains.

It seems like a harsh way to make the enemy fulfill the terms of surrender. Queen Isabella takes the child's hand, and the party of Moorish knights starts to ride back through the city gates.

They are about ten feet away from where you're standing when one of the Spanish knights appears to lose control of his horse. Something about the awkward way the poor knight is clinging to his horse's back tells you this is no knight—this is an Earth Inspector named Teega who's never been in a saddle before.

With growing horror you watch as the horse plunges into the group of Moorish knights. One of them is knocked from his saddle and another one grabs Teega's horse's reins.

The fallen knight picks himself up off the ground, removes a steel gauntlet from his hand, and throws it to the ground in front of Teega.

Amid the uproar, you're barely able to make out what happens next. But one thing's for sure: Teega has been challenged to a joust, and if you're to rescue her, you'd better come up with something fast!

Go on to the next page.

You dart through the crowd and grab the reins of Teega's mount, who is still excitedly prancing and whinnying.

"Whoa, there," you say to the horse. Then you send a thought transmission to the horse's rider: "Is that you in there, Teega?"

You immediately receive an excited reply. "Where'd *you* come from!"

Before you can answer, two of the Moorish knights appear on either side of Teega's horse. Your heart sinks. You suppose the Moors have been allowed to stay to make sure Teega doesn't try to get out of the joust. They'll be shadowing Teega to make sure she shows up. That means a quick exit is out of the question.

Your shadows lead the way to a makeshift jousting green at the edge of the city. One of them points to a small tent at one end of the green. You suppose it's for Teega's use until the joust begins.

Quickly a plan takes shape in your head. You tie up the horse and help Teega dismount. Then you lead her inside the tent.

The two of you communicate by thought waves.

"Teega, we've got to get you out of your armor."

"But what about the joust?"

"I don't have time to explain."

You help Teega remove her helmet and unbuckle the plates of armor. Then you start putting them on.

"Oh, no, I can't let you do this for me!" Teega says.

"At least I know how to ride a horse!" you say.

Once you're fully encased in the armor, you send another thought wave to Teega. "After I leave this tent, promise me you'll return to Turoc. I'll be right behind you as soon as I clean up a couple of odds and ends here."

Teega's blue-green Earthling eyes are full of tears. "Odds and ends! You could die out there!"

"My chances are a lot better than yours," you reply. In fact, she'd be facing certain death, but you decide it's better not to get into that discussion right now.

Teega sends a final thought wave. "Then go. And may the Power of Turoc go with you!"

Go on to the next page.

A few minutes later you're facing your opponent from one end of the grassy field. A good number of spectators are lined up along either side of the field.

You feel eerily calm, totally concentrating on what you're about to do. When the time comes, you lower the visor of your helmet, brace your lance against your body, aim it for your opponent's chest, and spur your horse into action.

Your horse gallops furiously toward the Moorish knight. You feel perfectly balanced in the high saddle, your iron feet secure in iron stirrups.

Your concentration is so heightened that everything seems to be happening in slow motion. Your opponent's lance is leveled, pointing toward your heart. He can't be more than thirty feet away—now twenty—now ten—

You feel a tremendous jolt as your lance hits the metal plate over his heart. You just keep going, feeling somewhat horrified at the idea that you've knocked him to the ground. But then you notice you're shaking with relief.

The crowd sends up a tremendous cheer. You trot over to your vanquished opponent.

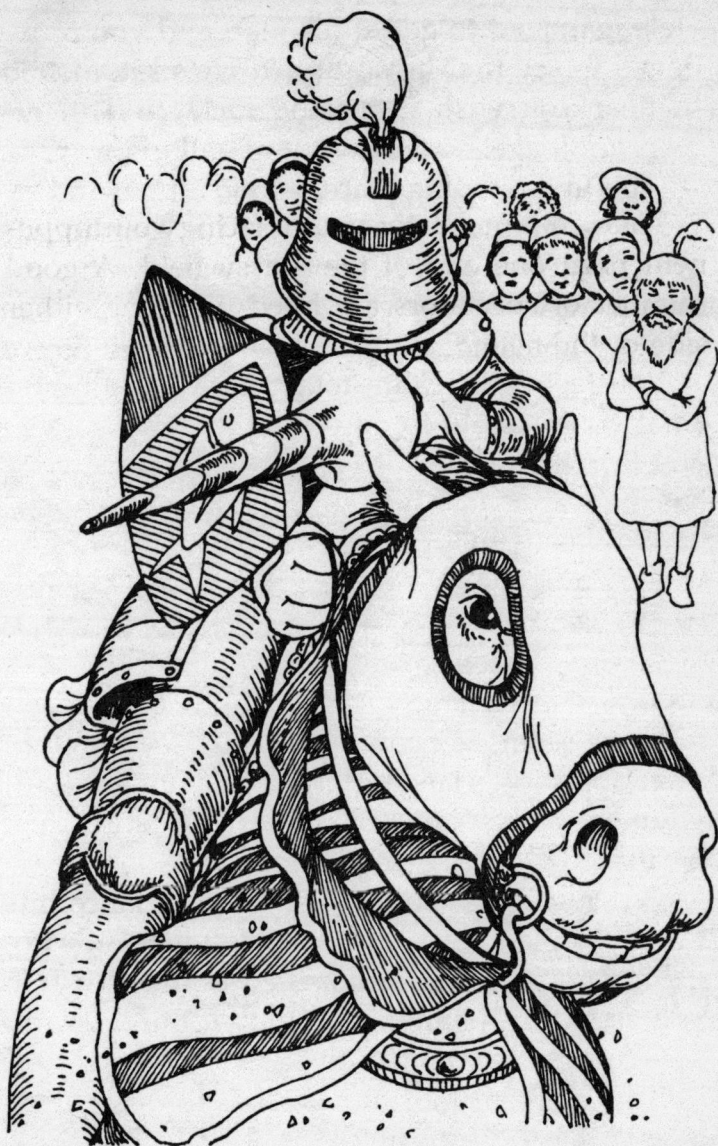

He's managed to get to his feet, and you're relieved to see that he's unhurt. He's astonished to hear you wish him good luck—and in his own language!—and then you gallop away.

You find a hiding place behind a barn and remove your armor. Then you remove your horse's armor and turn him out into a pasture with a pat on the rump. "We were a great team, but I'm afraid I'll have to say good-bye," you tell him.

Go on to the next page.

You decide to stay in the city until the Alhambra is finally surrendered. It's a dramatic moment when, some weeks later, King Boabdil rides out of the Alhambra and turns the keys to the castle over to King Ferdinand and Queen Isabella. Later, a silver cross will be mounted on a tower of the Alhambra. After 778 years, the Christians in Spain have finally succeeded in driving out the Muslims.

After the keys are surrended, Boabdil's son is returned to him. Everyone is touched to see the father take his son in his arms.

As you watch the elaborate ceremonies continue, you notice a man of about forty standing next to you. There's something familiar about his face.

You try to remember where you've seen him—and when you finally do remember, the answer comes as a pleasant shock. The face is indeed a famous one—or at least destined to become famous very soon. You recognize it from your Earth studies back on Turoc. It belongs to Christopher Columbus.

But why is he here?

The answer is supplied by Queen Isabella herself. After the surrender, she summons Columbus to her side and says, "Now, let's talk about this plan of yours to cross the ocean."

Wait'll you tell Simbar! You're standing next to one of the greatest of the Earth's own Earth Inspectors!

With a feeling of pride and happiness, you head toward your spacecraft, and home.

___

Turn to page 69.

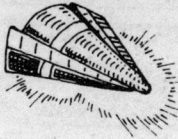

"Chin Chin, let's get out of here," you say.

"Where to, Inspector?" he asks.

"I don't know," you say. "But I do know we've got to watch our fuel supply. Just go into orbit while I figure out what to do," you tell him.

Once you're in orbit, Chin Chin shuts down the engines. It's so quiet you can almost hear yourself think, and it isn't long before you've come up with a plan.

"Chin Chin, get me to the year 2000," you say.

"But, Inspector, hardly any Earthlings live in castles in the year 2000," Chin Chin says. "And no one would capture a castle by building a city. Earthlings are equipped with such powerful weapons it wouldn't be necessary."

"I'm not looking for castles this time. I'm looking for information. The kind of information you get at a big university."

"Where do you want to go, then?"

"Let's try the city of Zurich, in Switzerland."

"Zurich it is," he says as he sets his coordinates.

As soon as Chin Chin is ready, you give the command: "Transit to the year 2000."

Turn to page 73.

Sara Compton has created hundreds of episodes of *Sesame Street* and other television shows, and is the recipient of five Emmys. She is the author of two other books in the EARTH INSPECTORS™ series, *Amazon* and *Venice*.

Mona Conner, a freelance illustrator, graduated from the School of Visual Arts in New York City. Her illustrations can be seen on many book covers and in magazines.

Barbara Carter is a freelance illustrator living in Randolph, Vermont.